MW00886579

# Mr. Pin

## and the
## Disappearing Diner

### VOL. VI

Other books by Mary Elise Monsell:

The Mysterious Cases of Mr. Pin

Mr. Pin: The Chocolate Files

The Spy Who Came North From the Pole

A Fish Named Yum

Mr. Pin and the Locked Diner Mystery

Crackle Creek

Toohy and Wood

Underwear

Armadillo

# Mr. Pin

## and the
## Disappearing Diner

### VOL. VI

**by Mary Elise Monsell**

**illustrated by Christina Cornier**

Mr. Pin and the Disappearing Diner, Vol. VI

Copyright © 2019 by Mary Elise Monsell

Illustrated by Christina Cornier

All rights reserved.
No part of this book may be reproduced or transmitted in any form or by any means, electronic, mechanical, photocopying, recording, or otherwise, without prior written permission of Mary Elise Monsell, except in the case of brief quotations embodied in critical articles or reviews.

Library of Congress Control Number: 2019908927

ISBN 978-0-9992787-1-0

# Dedications

For Lee and Marc

M.E.M. and Mr. Pin

For Emiliana

C.C.

# Acknowledgements

For the kindness and generosity of friends, not unlike those who visit Smiling Sally's Diner. Once again, many thanks to talented illustrator Christina Cornier, photographer Paul Lane, graphic artist Claudia Grosz, friends who helped edit, including Alice Blegen, Susan Green, and Domenica Cameron-Scorsese. Another big thank you to Laura Abbott for her editorial expertise.

## Author's Note

This book is a work of fiction. Any resemblance to actual people or penguins is truly a coincidence. They can be made real, of course, in your imagination.

# Mr. Pin

## and the
## Disappearing Diner

### VOL. VI

**by Mary Elise Monsell**

**illustrated by Christina Cornier**

# 1

Thundering applause filled the darkened Chicago theater. Slowly the curtain parted. A spot shone on a lone figure standing stage center.

Maggie and rockhopper penguin detective Mr. Pin watched as Mercury the Magician took a deep bow. Suddenly, he swirled his purple velvet cape and disappeared.

"I know that trick," said Mr. Pin to his friend Maggie. "I would tell you how it's done, but I have been sworn to secrecy."

Since fourteen-year-old Maggie had met the

rockhopper penguin years ago, he was always full

of surprises. "Where did you learn how to do it?"

asked Maggie.

"From another magician in Mexico," said Mr.

Pin. "He happened to tell me about Mercury. He

said the Chicago magician could make just about

anything disappear. Including himself."

"Interesting," said Maggie. "My theater

friends gave me these tickets to see Mercury's

show tonight."

Maggie didn't get a chance to ask Mr. Pin

any more questions about magic. Suddenly, her

phone lit up.

"It's Sally." The look on Maggie's face

changed from curiosity to concern.

"Mr. Pin, we have to hurry. Something is

terribly wrong. Aunt Sally just left me a message.

She said the diner has…DISAPPEARED!"

# 2

"Is Sally all right?" asked Mr. Pin, adjusting his checked cap and red muffler. He hopped toward the exit with Maggie at his side. First the magician vanished. Now the diner was gone! As if on cue, the theater's eerie organ music went along with his thoughts.

"Sally's message sounded serious," said Maggie. "She said she'd meet us on Monroe. That is, where the diner used to be."

It was unusual for Maggie to be so quiet as she and Mr. Pin rode the train south toward the only real home she had ever known. Both of Maggie's parents had mysteriously vanished while studying glaciers in Antarctica. Maggie was just a toddler when she came to live above the diner with her Aunt Sally.

For that matter, Smiling Sally's Diner had become Mr. Pin's second home and office as well, ever since he hopped off a bus at Wabash Street. He had come to Chicago to be a detective. Sally had told him he could stay in the diner's back room.

Maggie had been in elementary school about the same time Mr. Pin arrived. Since then, they became good friends and worked on many cases together. The penguin's first case in the Windy City was helping Sally. Gangsters had threatened to blow up her diner. But that was another story.

The train rolled to a stop, and Maggie and Mr. Pin hurried out the door and up the Red Line station stairs. Mr. Pin's long yellow plumes glistened in the cold rain.

As soon as the two turned the corner and looked down Monroe, both knew something was not right. There used to be a welcoming Smiling Sally's Diner sign. Now there was just a brick wall.

It was a dark, moonless night, but a familiar streetlight illumined an even darker truth.

The diner was gone!

The December wind blew Maggie's red hair in all directions, like the strong feelings that must be rising inside her. Her home had vanished! She spotted Sally pacing back and forth wringing her hands. Maggie looked even worse.

"I don't understand. I don't understand," Sally repeated.

Maggie hugged her aunt while Mr. Pin took a closer look. The diner windows, which used to show comfy booths, appeared to be walled over. Mr. Pin asked Maggie and her aunt the only question which made sense.

"When was the last time you saw the diner?" It was an unusual question, but this was an unusual case. It was as though the diner itself were a missing person.

"I've been away at school," said Maggie. "So a couple of weeks ago."

"This morning," said Sally. "I locked up and

went out to see holiday decorations. Closed the diner for the day. When I came back, the diner was gone. How can someone just steal a diner? And why?"

"I'm not sure, but I'm going to find out," said Mr. Pin. He wondered who knew Sally was closing the diner. From where he stood, casting a stout penguin shadow, he *did* know something was terribly wrong.

Maggie looked at her aunt with more concern. The wind was picking up and the air felt damp.

"We can't stay here. I'll call Uncle Otis." She was already entering her uncle's number. He lived in a large warehouse near the Chicago River. Otis sold odd parts rescued from demolished buildings.

Meanwhile, Sally kept shaking her head. Mr. Pin kept his as close to the ground as possible while still remaining upright. A flashlight, tucked under his wing, lit small cones of light on the sidewalk.

"Odd," he said more to himself than anyone else. He picked up a twisted shred of rope and put it into his black bag. Mr. Pin carried the mysterious bag everywhere. It had been all over the world on his many travels.

"That's him!" shouted Maggie. A van pulled up. "Uncle Otis!"

"That was quick," noted Mr. Pin out loud.

"So sorry to hear about the diner," said the driver.

A side door slid open, welcoming the

shivering group. Maggie took her aunt's hand and climbed in. Mr. Pin, who never got cold, took one last look around. Wishing he had more time, he turned off his flashlight and hopped in as well.

The van pulled away, but Mr. Pin had a sense of having missed a clue. Something was there. He just couldn't see it. Maybe he would get more answers in the daylight.

******

The warehouse looked much the same as Mr. Pin remembered it years before. There were pillars, door frames, old fireplaces, sconces, stained glass, even old theater parts, including a theater catwalk which had been taken apart.

"You still have gargoyles?" asked Maggie.

"Of course," said Uncle Otis who now walked with a cane.

Otis directed them to the elevator, which they all rode to an apartment on the third floor. When they stepped out of the elevator, they could see all of the various building parts from a balcony that stretched across the room. Statues and stone gargoyles stared back as they advanced down the creaking metal walkway.

Uncle Otis opened a hand-carved door, salvaged from an old theater, revealing his cozy apartment. Sally and Maggie sat together on a green velvet couch with scrolled wood arms. Uncle Otis took their coats and hung them in a gigantic armoire. Then he headed for a small kitchen to make something hot.

Mr. Pin was quiet even as Uncle Otis set hot chocolate by his outstretched wing.

Maggie spoke for everyone.

"Thank you for letting us stay here, Uncle Otis. I'll help you with making up beds. We should leave a note on the diner wall in the morning. I mean, where the diner used to be. How could it disappear?" Maggie had a way of talking all at once.

"I just don't understand," said Sally.

"Don't worry," said Maggie. "We'll find it. Mr. Pin and I are on the case."

"I know, dear. Mr. Pin has always helped, even when the diner was almost blown up."

"Mr. Pin has helped a lot of people," said Maggie. "And you have always helped whenever people needed you, including me." Maggie gave her aunt a hug.

"It was easy to help you," said Sally to her niece. Changing the subject, she asked, "How was the magic show?"

"Fantastic!" said Maggie. "Even Mercury the Magician disappeared during the curtain call."

"Mercury?" asked Uncle Otis. "He came by here the other day."

"How exciting," said Maggie. "What did he get?"

"A scaffold, stage lights," said Otis as he pulled a Murphy bed down from the wall.

"Scaffold?" asked Mr. Pin, his plumes rising in interest. "Fascinating." A vague thought floated through his feathered head. He had seen a scaffold somewhere else. It was helpful when laying bricks to make a wall....

Sally and Maggie soon settled into a spare room while Mr. Pin paced back and forth. It would be much later before he would finally sleep for a few fitful hours on the Murphy bed. Uncle Otis could be heard snoring from his room in the small apartment. Mr. Pin's thoughts seemed louder as he kept thinking about coincidences, magicians, and scaffolds. And not too far from his thoughts was the memory of a previous case which involved falling gargoyles. There were still gargoyles in Uncle Otis's warehouse. And there was still a spy named Gargoyle who became infamous in The Spy Who Came North From the Pole. Could he be involved in the diner's disappearance?

******

It was well past midnight when a short figure hopped down Monroe Street into the now-sleeting night. The city slept, but not Mr. Pin. Not minding the cold, the penguin detective carefully hung a sign on the wall where the diner once stood:

**Smiling Sally's Diner is closed due to its disappearance. Anyone who has information or knows where it might be, please contact Mr. Pin at Otis Salvage Warehouse. Sally hopes to be back in business as soon as her diner is found.**

# 3

Sally wanted to return to the scene of the disappearing diner early in the morning.

"We need to let people know," said Sally.

"No problem," said Mr. Pin. "I put up a sign last night. I knew you would be worried about your customers."

Sally gave Mr. Pin a wide smile. She still insisted on seeing the spot where her diner had once been. With great concern and without breakfast, they rode in Uncle Otis's van.

When they turned the corner onto Monroe,

Maggie practically shrieked. "It's back!"

Everyone jumped out to see the same, wonderful old diner still there in one piece, just as it had always been. The brick wall was gone. So was Mr. Pin's sign.

"Something is very strange about this," said Mr. Pin. There was little time to think about that.

The next few hours were a bit of a blur as everyone hurried to open the diner for the morning rush. Mr. Pin flipped pancakes. Maggie brought out cinnamon rolls, and Sally poured coffee. The diner was packed with truck drivers, Maggie's drama club friends, opera singers, office workers and, interestingly, Mercury the Magician. Even Sergeant O'Malley was there.

"Say, I heard you lost the diner," said the

whiskered sergeant.

"It vanished," said Mercury, taking the cue. "Into thin air." He made a dramatic gesture to show something disappearing.

"I was going to file a missing diner report," O'Malley went on. "But I see that you found it. The diner, that is."

Mr. Pin just kept flipping pancakes, but from the corner of his red eye, he noticed O'Malley's fleeting smile. *What did he know?*

After the morning rush settled, Maggie and Mr. Pin finally ate breakfast. Sally's smile was back. In fact, everything in the diner looked exactly the same. Everything. It was almost as if nothing had happened. Except it did. And if the diner disappeared once, perhaps it could disappear again. Even if O'Malley didn't quite take this seriously, Mr. Pin certainly did. He kept thinking about that as he poured syrup onto his chocolate chip pancakes.

"Been here long?" Mercury asked. He was sitting to Mr. Pin's left. Maggie was on the penguin's right.

"I was here for several years until I needed to help out in South America. A spy was causing trouble. I came back when I found out the diner might need me."

"Mr. Pin was chasing spies right here in Chicago!" said Maggie. "He came back here just in time."

"That happens a lot with Mr. Pin," said Sally. "Helping just in time, that is."

For just a second, Mr. Pin looked up as Sally spoke. When he picked up his fork, something was missing. Chocolate chip pancakes!

"They're gone!" said Mr. Pin, sounding almost excited, which never happened.

The penguin detective studied the magician sitting next to him. Mercury was slowly eating a cinnamon roll and sipping coffee. His eyebrows rose in a tall arch when he noticed the penguin eyeing him. Then he laughed.

"I should have known I couldn't fool Chicago's most famous detective." Smiling, the magician revealed Mr. Pin's original plate of pancakes hidden beneath a newspaper.

*Diabolical. Did the magician know just how important chocolate was to him?*

Sighing, Mr. Pin returned to his chocolate chip pancakes and the case at hand. "A diner just doesn't walk away," he said out loud.

"That's right," said Maggie to Mercury. "The diner disappeared and then came back this morning. Maybe you have some ideas how that could happen."

"Sounds like a good illusion," said Mercury to Maggie and Mr. Pin. "You know, mystery and magic have a lot in common. Speaking of which, you should come to my magic shop."

"I'd like that," said Mr. Pin.

"Splendid," said Mercury. His dark eyebrows rose again as he clasped his hands together like a tent.

Mr. Pin studied the mysterious magician.

He wondered, as he had another bite of pancake,

whether Mercury was creating a distraction.

Magicians did that a lot. He would find out soon

enough.

# 4

"I have never been to a magic shop before," said Maggie to her friend Mr. Pin. Maggie and Mr. Pin were riding in a taxi to the North Side. Mr. Pin nodded. He knew he didn't have to answer. Maggie just liked to think out loud.

As the taxi pulled up in front of Mercury's Magic Emporium, Maggie said, "According to Mercury, many magicians come here."

The shop was tucked away in a brick building. A few stairs took them down into the shop. Maggie and Mr. Pin looked around by themselves. No owner was in sight. Yet, it appeared that there was more in the shop than met the eye. A glass counter stood in front of a long wall of unlabeled drawers. One could only guess what was inside each one.

On the opposite side, there was a wall of books about magic. Mr. Pin started to read the titles, especially the ones on illusions, when Mercury came out from a back room.

"Are there any specific tricks about making a place disappear?" asked Mr. Pin.

"It sounds like an interesting piece of magic," said Mercury.

"It wasn't gone for long," said Maggie. "The diner, that is."

Mr. Pin noticed that the magician didn't

really answer his question about making a place disappear. He just said it was interesting. Then he changed the subject.

"Here, let me show you a card trick." The magician's hands moved quickly, spreading cards like a little dance. "Take a card."

Maggie pulled a nine of hearts out of the deck.

"Remember the card. Don't show me. Now put it back into the deck."

Mercury shuffled the cards and slowly spread them out.

"Is this your card?" It was the nine of hearts.

"That's great! Can I buy that card trick?" asked Maggie.

"Of course," said Mercury. Buying a trick

meant being told its secret solution. He opened one of the drawers and pulled out another deck of cards.

While the magician showed Maggie the trick, Mr. Pin looked around the shop. He didn't know what he was looking for exactly, but he thought he had found a clue just as Mercury was wrapping up the sale. When he hopped back to the counter, Mr. Pin kept his "find" to himself. Still, he had to ask a question.

"*Why* do you think someone made the diner disappear?"

The magician tented his fingers again and spoke softly.

"Perhaps it is not a crime."

"Perhaps," said Mr. Pin.

On their way out, Mr. Pin noticed theater lights and part of a metal scaffold leaning against a wall. Mercury's shoulders shrugged as if in response.

"A lot is needed for a magic show," said the magician.

An idea was forming in Mr. Pin's mind as he and his friend Maggie rode back to the diner. He was still stuck with why anyone would go to so much trouble just to make a building disappear. Then reappear. He wasn't getting much information from the magician. And why did he find a piece of rope in the magic shop, much like the rope he had found outside the diner? He kept both pieces of rope in his black bag.

******

Much later, in Mr. Pin's back room office, the penguin detective attached a large sheet of paper to the wall. He wrote **Suspects** at the top of the sheet. Wide-eyed, Maggie watched as he wrote the name **Mercury.**

"I can see why you would think of him," said Maggie. "He does make things disappear. Magicians *are* mysterious. And this is certainly a mystery. I have only one question. How could he make the diner disappear and be at his own show at the same time?"

"Very good question," said Mr. Pin. "Perhaps the magician taking a bow wasn't Mercury."

"Perhaps," said Maggie. "He sure looked like Mercury."

Then Mr. Pin wrote another name on his

sheet of paper. **Otis.**

"Uncle Otis?" asked Maggie. "Why in the world is Uncle Otis a suspect?"

"He came by the diner awfully fast after you called him. Almost like he was expecting trouble."

"Hard to imagine Uncle Otis making a diner disappear."

"True," said Mr. Pin.

"Here's where I'm stuck," the rockhopper went on. "Motivation."

"You mean *why* would someone do it?"

"Exactly."

"Good question," said Maggie.

"Was it some kind of distraction?" asked the penguin detective.

"For what?" asked Maggie.

"Could he be hiding a greater crime?" Mr. Pin clearly valued her opinion.

"Does Mercury seem like the kind of person who would commit a crime?" asked his friend.

"Hard to say," said Mr. Pin.

"Can you call it a crime if someone makes something disappear, like a diner, but then brings it back?" asked Maggie.

"Another good point," said Mr. Pin. Maggie had many talents, one of them being her logical, scientific mind.

Just then a truck rumbled down the alley and screeched to a halt by the back door.

"Delivery?" asked Maggie.

"Possibly," said Mr. Pin. "Pretty late for that."

Mr. Pin motioned with his wing to the back door. He looked through its small peep hole. A van with smudged letters was parked just outside. The motor was running. Maggie looked next.

"I'm not sure, but it looks like a produce truck," said Maggie.

"Look again," said Mr. Pin.

"No! It can't be," said Maggie. "Is that Uncle Otis?"

"And why is he delivering vegetables?" asked Mr. Pin.

"Hit the lights!" The two detectives hid behind the door of Mr. Pin's office. Maggie tossed a large burlap bag over her head. In the dark, they could both hear the back door lock being picked.

"Does your uncle know how to pick locks?"

whispered Mr. Pin.

"I don't think so," Maggie whispered back.

"Could be someone else."

The question was who.

Someone wanted them to think it was Uncle Otis in case they spotted the truck.

Just then the diner's back door slowly opened. It was not Uncle Otis. There was no familiar tapping of a cane. Mr. Pin raised his wing to his beak to signal quiet while grasping a heavy rag mop. He was ready for trouble.

There were a few thumps and bumps and then the sound of the back door closing again. Both raced out of Mr. Pin's office. Mr. Pin quickly set the bolt.

Piled high near the back door were several

boxes of lettuce, carrots, onions, and potatoes.

"Why would someone sneak in to deliver vegetables?" asked Maggie.

"Look again," said Mr. Pin.

Maggie took a few bunches of carrots and put them on Mr. Pin's desk. Underneath were theater lights. Other boxes held pulleys, cords, and curtains.

"This case is getting more curious by the moment," said Mr. Pin.

Then he noticed one more thing inside his office. On his desk was a jar of what looked like stage makeup.

"I wonder if one of my friends left that," volunteered Maggie. "They came by here the other morning."

"But why would they leave it in the back room?" asked Mr. Pin. "And why are there theater supplies in boxes by the back door?"

Maggie watched in alarm while Mr. Pin wrote **Maggie's Drama Club Friends** under the heading of **Suspects**.

"I'd like to talk to your friends," said Mr. Pin. "I am curious about the stage makeup. And we should talk to Mercury again. These lights are similar to the ones I saw in his shop."

Mr. Pin thought Mercury knew more than he was saying. As it turned out, the truth and a magician who knew it could prove difficult to find.

# 5

The next morning, Maggie said she had a day off from school. She needed to write up a science lab. After that, her friends were stopping by the diner.

"Are these your drama club friends?" asked Mr. Pin.

"Yes. They love the cinnamon rolls."

"Understandable. Please ask them about the theater supplies we found in the back room."

"Of course," said Maggie.

Sally said she wanted to make a delivery to

a food pantry.

"My friends and I can help out here," said Maggie to her aunt.

"Okay, thanks. One of the truckers said he would be here, too," said Sally.

That left Mr. Pin with the Mercury visit.

It just happened that Luigi the pasta maker was driving by in his truck as Mr. Pin was raising his wing for a cab. Mr. Pin thought they were seeing a lot of old friends lately. A lot of friends who showed up when needed.

"Can I give you a ride?" asked Luigi.

"Thanks," said Mr. Pin. "I'm going to a magic shop."

"Hop in," said Luigi.

Mr. Pin was just thinking about how nice the

truck smelled with scents of chocolate and tomato sauce when he spotted a flash of purple. Luigi pulled his truck up in front of Mercury's Magic Emporium. At that very moment, Mercury was leaving by another door.

Mr. Pin waved his wings, drawing the attention of everyone except Mercury. The magician stepped into a taxi. At least, Mr. Pin thought it was the magician. Mostly what he saw was his cape.

"No problem," said Luigi to the rockhopper. "You want me to follow that taxi?"

"And the purple cape," said Mr. Pin. "Thank you."

The taxi soon headed down Lake Shore Drive toward Adler Planetarium, then made a quick exit toward the parking garage. Mercury got out of the taxi. Mr. Pin hopped out of the truck and headed toward the magician. Before he could reach him, Mercury got into another taxi. Fortunately, Luigi stayed put. Mr. Pin got back into Luigi's pasta truck.

"I wonder if he is avoiding me," said Mr. Pin.

"Seems to be the case. You still want me to follow the magician in the purple cape?" asked Luigi.

Mr. Pin nodded.

"There's a problem," said Luigi. "It looks like two magicians, two purple capes, and two taxis."

"Follow that one," said Mr. Pin pointing to the one farther away. Pure penguin instinct.

"Sure thing," said Luigi.

The taxi Mr. Pin had chosen veered north

again and raced down Lower Wacker Drive. Luigi's truck careened around corners as the car they were following seemed to be making a magical tour of the city, disappearing and then suddenly reappearing. Just then, the taxi made a sharp turn and zoomed up a ramp into a high rise building. Luigi held up his hand.

"I'm sorry, Mr. Pin. My truck is too tall for that garage."

"That's all right," said the detective. "I'll see if I can follow on foot."

Mr. Pin hopped out and headed for the lobby on two webbed feet. From the corner of his red eye, he spotted a familiar cape. He hopped after the cape into a lobby chocolate shop.

"Diabolical," muttered Mr. Pin. "He knows I

would lose my concentration here." After sampling a piece of dark chocolate and one hazelnut seashell, Mr. Pin looked around and realized the cape was fluttering by an open back door. This time, no one was in it. It was hanging on a hook.

"Do you know if this has been here long?" asked Mr. Pin.

"I have never seen that cape before," said the man behind the counter.

"Is it all right if I use your back door?" asked Mr. Pin.

"Go right ahead, and please take some chocolate with you. I have never met anyone who likes my chocolate as much as you." The man smiled and handed Mr. Pin a bag of chocolate pieces.

Mr. Pin hopped down the alley. He wasn't sure which direction to take until he spotted fresh footprints in the snow. He followed them until they disappeared when they met the sidewalk. Mr. Pin sighed, consoled only by the contents of the white paper bag.

Luigi's familiar truck was parked nearby.

"I suppose I shouldn't be surprised that a magician is good at disappearing," said Mr. Pin to Luigi.

"He is good at being many places at once," agreed the pasta maker. "Maybe he has an assistant."

"Or maybe more than one cape," said Mr. Pin. "He even left one hanging on a hook in a chocolate shop." Mr. Pin was beginning to get another idea.

"Perhaps there was always only one magician, but two capes in two taxis. Mercury might have left a cape on a hook in a taxi to make me believe he was in it. That's how he could be in two places at once."

"Excellent idea," said Luigi. "And he knows you very well." Luigi pointed to the chocolate Mr. Pin was eating.

"It is the ultimate distraction," said Mr. Pin, not unhappily.

"Why would he lead you on such a chase?" asked Luigi.

"Good question," said Mr. Pin. "It makes me wonder what he could be up to."

The question hung in the air along with

the captivating scents of chocolate and tomato sauce. Luigi turned down Monroe, the same street Smiling Sally's Diner was on. Or where it used to be. Mr. Pin's red eyes froze, riveted to a familiar brick wall. His worst fears had been realized. The diner had disappeared again!

# 6

Each one of Mr. Pin's feathers seemed to stand on end.

Mercury! He was the diner thief! It had to be him! But where was the magician? And just what did he do with the diner? Where were Maggie and her friends? They had been inside. But the person Mr. Pin saw next wasn't the magician. It was Otis.

"Otis?" asked Mr. Pin in a state of rare shock. Maggie's uncle was standing near the wall holding a long rope.

"Hello, Mr. Pin. How are you?" asked Otis,

leaning on his cane. "As you will soon see, I'm kind of good with pulleys, ropes, and, of course, elevators. That's why they put me in charge of lifting and lowering the wall, with some electrical assistance. The drama club designed the whole thing."

"Wall? Maggie's friends?" asked Mr. Pin.

"Right. You found part of the rope near the diner and in the magic shop."

"How did you know?"

"Mercury told me. We're working together."

"Working together to make the diner disappear! You and Mercury?" asked Mr. Pin, stunned.

"That's right. It was necessary. Mercury had to do a show. That left me in charge of the wall. He managed to get back here to help at just the right moment. Anyway, that's why I was nearby when you needed a ride to my warehouse."

"But Sally..."

"It is all for Sally...and you. In a moment you will see for yourself. Not all mysteries are crimes."

That's when Mr. Pin noticed the scaffold in a narrow gap between the buildings, rising high above where the diner used to be. There was a familiar purple flash and the hum of a motor. Otis signaled to the magician above while he gripped a rope to slowly guide what happened next.

And then the strangest thing took place.

The brick wall shuddered and swayed with an eerie mechanical moan.Then, slowly, very slowly the wall rolled up like a window shade.

Mercury was operating a device on top of a scaffold and carefully making the diner reappear. It was hidden from the street. Mr. Pin was seldom astonished, but it all started to make sense.

Mercury must have been helping Otis make the diner disappear while it seemed the magician was taking a bow. Only it was just an empty purple velvet cape vanishing into an opening in the stage floor. At that point, Mercury was long gone. No one was actually in the cape. Just like the chocolate shop and the taxi. It was all a great illusion.

Luigi parked in an alley as Sally showed up with one of the truckers. Sally ran over to Mr. Pin.

"I think we should go inside," said Mr. Pin to Sally. "This is a little unusual."

Both penguin and diner owner would long remember this day. Even the most famous Chicago detective could not have imagined what was about to happen next. Mr. Pin never stuck around for a "thank you" after solving a case. Sally was much the same in her own way whenever she helped someone out. This time they both had no choice.

# 7

The diner was transformed. Maggie's theater friends had been quite busy. So had a lot of other people. Stage lights outlined the ceiling. Rows and rows of chairs had been brought in. Mr. Pin was greeted by one of Maggie's friends who had two long yellow plumes highlighting her own braided black hair. She wore a jacket that looked much like penguin wings. Another friend wore a long apron and had her hair cropped short like Smiling Sally.

Then, without warning, booths suddenly swiveled and opened to reveal the rest of Maggie's

friends, all in costume, as well as just about everyone Mr. Pin and Sally knew. All of them—from a conductor named Al, to Luigi who liked to sing in his truck, to a baseball manager, to folks who had gotten free food from Sally, to museum directors, and even to Sergeant O'Malley—had been helped in some way by either the penguin detective or Maggie's aunt. The most surprising magic was how much Mr. Pin and Sally had done for people in the Windy City. The diner itself had been transformed into a stage for a play honoring Sally and Mr. Pin.

Maggie came out from the swinging doors and greeted the astounded pair.

"You were in on this?" asked Mr. Pin.

"I had to be. We all had to do something

to surprise you and Sally. You have helped so many people in Chicago. We wanted to thank you. Especially me."

"I don't know what to say," said Sally.

"And I'm so sorry if I worried you," said Maggie to her aunt.

"I do understand," said Sally as she hugged her niece.

"Clever illusion," said Mr. Pin to Mercury who had just come through the main door in his purple velvet cape. "It seems you have been many places at once."

"I do have more than one cape," said Mercury. "I am sorry I led you on such a chase. You see it was necessary to create the time to make this happen." Then, to both Sally and Mr.

Pin, he said, "Now, if you would, please take your honored seats as we present a play celebrating all you have done for so many people in your very wonderful lives. As Sally says, no reason why big cities can't have big hearts."

Let the play begin...

# Mr. Pin

## and the
## Disappearing Diner
## PLAY

## Author's Note

Based on the Mr. Pin mystery series, the play is designed to be performed in a classroom. Some parts are flexible, so everyone can participate. For example, Maggie's character can be played by one or two students. She first appears briefly as a two-year-old. The same actress transforms into an eight-year-old and then into a fourteen-year-old. Or, yet another student can play the part of the fourteen-year-old Maggie.

As guests of honor, Sally and Mr. Pin sit in the "audience" and then become part of the play itself. The acting friends and truckers might double as part of the chorus, etc.

Staging can be quite simple or more elaborate depending on preference. Most classrooms don't have spotlights, but perhaps a lamp or flashlight could be used.

The play opens as the book itself ends: in the diner. Friends are gathered to honor Mr. Pin and Sally. Students can be sitting or standing by desks. With a few diner cups and an old "radio," the scene will come alive.

# THE CAST

The radio (old radio prop or actor playing the radio)

Sally

Sergeant O'Malley

Maggie

Chorus

Mr. Pin

Truckers

Picasso thief

Policeman

Professor Hugo Femur

Berta Largamente

Alberto Dente

Luigi

Walter Wavemin

Sam Spitter

Mercury

Otis

# MR. PIN AND THE DISAPPEARING DINER
## PLAY

*Scene opens with the diner dark, and a "spotlight" is focused on an older radio (or student). Sally gets up from her seat and turns on the radio. She starts arranging diner cups and saucers while listening to the announcer.*

Radio:       Two Chicago scientists, who were working in Antarctica, have disappeared. No further information is available. Sally, sister of one of the scientists, says she will not give up hope that they will be found. Meanwhile, their little girl, Maggie, will stay with her Aunt Sally, owner of a diner on Monroe. The aunt hopes the family will one day be reunited.

*There is a knock on the diner door. Sally opens it and lets in a very young Maggie with Sergeant O'Malley. She is carrying a small suitcase and a stuffed penguin. She hugs her aunt and exits to the side with Sally. Perhaps a bit of music indicates a time change or the room darkens briefly. The very young Maggie actress quickly returns as an older Maggie (about eight). She sounds as though she has come running down the stairs two at a time. She is also carrying a stuffed penguin. Sally takes a seat in the audience, close to the front. The lights go on.*

Eight-year-old Maggie: *(singing center stage)*
> You've been there for me, Aunt Sally,
> When I needed you, Aunt Sally,
> You took care of me,
> Since I was two.
> Without you, what would I do?
> You gave me gerbils,
> A CB radio,
> And you combed my curls.
> Made me cinnamon rolls,
> Oh, when I was all alone.
> You gave me a home, Aunt Sally.
> You've always been there, Aunt Sally.
> You took care of me, Aunt Sally,
> Since I was two.
> Without you, what would I do?

Sally:  I had help you know. *(Maggie sits next to Sally.)*

Chorus:  Mr. Pin. Ra-da-da-da-da-da-da.
He's on the case. *(whispered)*
Mr. Pin. Ra-da-da-da-da-da-da.

He's on the case. *(whispered)*
Mr. Pin. Ra-da-da-da-da-da-da.
He's on the case. *(whispered)*
*(possible dance routine)*

Mr. Pin:     *(Gets up and reminisces from the front of the "stage")*
I got off a bus at Wabash St. The bus headed west. I headed north. I was at home in Chicago. It was cold.
*(He turns on the radio.)*

Radio:     This just in. A rock hit a streetlight. Glass splintered. Almost broke the window of Smiling Sally's Diner on Monroe. *(sound effect)* A black car squealed away.

Mr. Pin:     *(picking up a rock and reading an attached note):* "Pay up or else." I wonder if that rock was meant for the diner. Smiling Sally's Diner. Hmm. Lights are on. Looks like it's open.

Sally:     *(Standing)* Come on in. Make yourself at home. This is my place, so I do what I want. Food's good and you meet interesting people. Say, you don't look like you're from around here.

| | |
|---|---|
| Mr. Pin: | Detective Pin. I travel a lot, but I'm from the South Pole. |
| Sally: | Want something cold? |
| Mr. Pin: | I like ice cream, especially chocolate. |
| Sally: | Coming right up. No charge. |
| Mr. Pin: | *(To the audience)* We became friends right away. |
| O'Malley: | Sally's like that. |
| Sally: | It was during that first case when Mr. Pin met my niece. |

*Eight-year-old Maggie gets up and sets the stuffed penguin on the counter when she sees Mr. Pin, the real deal.*

| | |
|---|---|
| Maggie: | I needed a good friend at about that time. |
| Sally: | Maggie's always been busy. She's interested in everything. |
| Maggie: | I like learning. Hanging around a penguin detective gives me a lot to think about. Mr. Pin taught me how to dust for fingerprints. (*Maggie could pantomime fingerprint dusting or* |

*actually do it.)*

Sally: It's a skill every little girl should know. Anyway, Maggie helped Mr. Pin with that first case and many others. Glad I got her a citizen's band radio. Came in handy.

Maggie: I used that cb radio to talk to the truckers on the highway.

Mr. Pin: Good to have friends on the road.

Maggie: They showed up with lots of ice cream. Mr. Pin came up with a trick to trap the gangsters.

Mr. Pin: I am a nonviolent penguin. I prefer ice cream.

Maggie: Everyone helped with that case.

Sally: That's the way it works. The diner might not have survived without Mr. Pin and the diner family. (She nods toward the truckers.)

A trucker: People come to Smiling Sally's Diner for help. We are grateful to you, Sally and Mr. Pin…for everything you've done.

Another trucker: Sally's always giving away free
food, lending a hand.

*Sally could fill a bag with groceries and give it to
someone in the audience. She might also give
someone else a coat.*

Maggie:         Speaking of food, Mr. Pin, tell everyone
                about the Picasso thief. Do you
                remember the extra-large, chocolate
                wedding cake?

Mr. Pin:        How could I forget?

Radio:          Breaking story. Picasso's famous
                *Old Guitarist* was stolen from the
                Art Institute. The thief created an
                exploding flour balloon diversion.

*Actor holds a framed painting as though it's
hanging on a wall. Picasso thief tiptoes toward
the painting. The thief could use some device,
like confetti, and throws it up into the air as a
distraction. The thief takes the painting from the
actor. He trips over Mr. Pin who looks right at him.
The thief runs away. Mr. Pin checks the imaginary
wall or person pretending to be the wall where the
painting once hung. He preens his wing.*

Mr. Pin:        Hmm. Chocolate.

Chorus:      *(whispering)* He's on the case.

O'Malley:    Can you describe the thief who tripped over your beak?

Mr. Pin:     He had green eyes and probably likes chocolate.

O'Malley:    Did he get a look at you?

Mr. Pin:     He knows I'm a penguin.

Policeman:   I remember that case well with, uh, Detective Pin... A lot of bakeries were involved.

Maggie:      We had to find the stolen painting.

O'Malley:    Pretty clever thief.

Mr. Pin:     Research was essential. I had to match the chocolate I discovered on the museum wall. It was an important clue.

Policeman:   We drove all over Chicago.

O'Malley:    You are truly a chocolate expert, Mr. Pin. Say, the Art Institute wasn't the only museum where one of your cases took place.

Maggie:      We stumbled on a crime of chocolate

at the Field Museum. Really hot that day. Professor Femur?

**Professor:** Did you know we found fossilized baby dinosaurs inside Protoceratops eggs? Glad you were there, Mr. Pin.

**Chorus:** *(whispered)* He's on the case.

**Radio:** While Chicago sizzles, The Field Museum is the scene of a baffling crime. Dinosaur eggs were stolen and replaced by …chocolate eggs! The museum was plunged into darkness. Penguin detective Mr. Pin was on hand …or wing…once again to test the chocolate. Unfortunately…

**Maggie:** Bad chocolate in those eggs.

**Mr. Pin:** Made me sick. Maggie took over the case.

**Chorus Song:**

> Bad chocolate is always a crime.
> Bad chocolate is always a crime
> Never ever eat the stuff; it's filled with grit.
> Bad chocolate is always a crime.

Maggie: *(to Sally)* You stood by me when I needed help with "The case of eggs." *(Sally gives her niece a hug.)*

Sally: Always.

Mr. Pin: Sally, you were there when I was recovering in the back room of the diner...from bad chocolate.

Berta Largamente: Excuse me. I hate to interrupt, but that reminds me about me. Mr. Pin solved an important problem at the opera house. I was so worried about the conductor. I thought he was going to be kidnapped. It would have been disaster for my show. My solos. My career. That penguin is a marvel with mystery.

Radio: This just in. Lyric Opera conductor has disappeared in cloud of blue smoke.

Berta: Alberto Dente, the conductor. He likes being called Mac. *(Mac is sitting nearby. He rises and taps a baton on a cart. He raises both arms to conduct).*

Chorus: *(whispered)* ra-da-da-da-da-da-da.

| | |
|---|---|
| Conductor: | Always wanted to drive a truck. Not easy if your job is conducting opera. |
| Luigi: | I wanted to sing in the opera. |
| Conductor: | I found my truck, thanks to Mr. Pin. |
| Luigi: | A certain penguin detective helped me find my voice. |
| Berta: | Of course. Of course. Mr. Pin did assist you with your vocal career. My career was, of course, perfect. Now, Luigi sings in his truck with occasional international appearances as a star tenor. Luigi also makes delicious pasta and chocolate. |
| Luigi: | Only the best. Chocolate and pasta. |
| Conductor: | Mr. Pin brings out the best in people. |
| Berta: | Were you aware that *Mr. Pin* also conducts music? |
| Chorus: | *(a little louder)* ra-da-da-da-da-da-da-da. He's on the case. |
| Maggie: | My friend Mr. Pin knows a lot of things. He has studied music, fossils, plants, art, forensics, baseball. |

Walter Wavemin *(in Cubs teeshirt):* That's right. Mr. Pin is a good catcher. Throws well, too. Nice wing on that penguin. Especially when he has a frosty malt in his other wing.

Mr. Pin: There are no minor leagues at the South Pole. Had to be good to play baseball in Antarctica. Growing up, that is.

Radio: The Dodgers are up at bat. Runners are in the corners. And the game is tied 5 to 5, top of the seventh. Cubs are in the field.

Mr. Pin: Strange. There's a note on this frosty malt lid. It's from Walter Wavemin. He needs help.

Maggie: Walter is the Cubs manager. He likes to wave 'em in. The runners, that is. *(Walter makes the point by waving his arms enthusiastically.)*

Mr. Pin: Interesting case of disguise and identity. The Spitter Pitchers. Two brothers. Both played baseball.

Maggie: You helped me with my fastball, Mr. Pin.

Mr. Pin: Just keep your fingers on the seams.

Berta: Would you like to hear me sing "The Star Spangled Banner?"

Sam Spitter: You helped my brother get a shot at the majors.

Walter Wavemin: I still wouldn't mind signing you on, Mr. Pin.

Mr. Pin: Thanks. But Maggie's the one who has a fantastic fastball. Besides, I may have my most important case yet.

O'Malley: Say, Mr. Pin, speaking of cases, remember, we thought you might be having a crime spree in Chicago. *(loud crash, like falling books.)*

Radio: Has Chicago's famous detective gone wrong? Someone spotted a rockhopper penguin near the scene of a crime. Not only that, an empty box of chocolate was found near the shattered remains of smashed gargoyles.

| | |
|---|---|
| Mr. Pin: | It was a dark time. |
| O'Malley: | I took you off the case. |
| Mr. Pin: | Not for long. |
| Chorus: | *(maybe standing with arms crossed)* He's on the case. |
| Maggie: | I never believed Mr. Pin was the gargoyle smasher. He had to clear his name. I thought it might be a trap, so somehow I forgot that Mr. Pin told me not to get involved. That's when Sally gave me my favorite breakfast to help me think. A pancake sandwich. Pancakes on the outside. Eggs on the inside. Sally's the best. |

*Sally hands out sandwiches to random people.*

| | |
|---|---|
| Mr. Pin: | Turns out there was a spy named Gargoyle. |
| Maggie: | An actual spy. He came north from the South Pole. |
| Mr. Pin: | Later on, I followed Gargoyle to another continent. He was causing a lot of trouble. |

| | |
|---|---|
| Maggie: | Mr. Pin was gone for a long time. We missed him. But I had my Aunt Sally. Always. And Mr. Pin had taught me that I could do anything. |
| Mr. Pin: | I had to track down Gargoyle and an important lead. |
| Maggie: | You got a mysterious message bringing you back to Chicago. By then, I was fourteen. *(Note: eight-year-old Maggie could exit and another actor could play the fourteen-year-old Maggie.)* |
| Mr. Pin: | I thought the diner might be in trouble. You had become quite good as a detective while I was gone. |
| Maggie: | I like looking for clues to solve mysteries. You showed me how to do that. And you taught me how to decipher codes. |
| Mr. Pin: | There were a couple of them in The Locked Diner Mystery. |
| Maggie: | You had another close call in that case, as I remember. Someone had gotten into the diner, committed a crime |

when it was bolted from the inside. An almost impossible mystery to solve.

Mr. Pin:     Almost.

Maggie:      You believed in me, Mr. Pin right from the start. You told me about forensics.

Mr. Pin:     You are a natural detective.

Chorus:      She's on the case.

Mercury:     Excuse me. While we're on the subject of interesting people, I'd like to talk about magic. Let's make something disappear. Or perhaps you'd like me to read your mind. I can do that too.

Sally:       Just what did you have in mind?

Radio:       This just in. We have learned that famous Smiling Sally's Diner on Monroe has disappeared. Rockhopper penguin detective Mr. Pin is on the case. Mercury, a famous magician, is a prime suspect.

Mercury:     *(The magician could act out some of these or other tricks as he sings):*
             I'm Mercury the Magician
             I can read your mind.

I'm Mercury the Magician
I can pull rabbits out of hats
Hats out of rabbit pockets
Pockets out of hats
Pockets out of pockets
Card tricks, scarf tricks, coin tricks,
And of course, disappearing diners.

Mr. Pin: *(to Mercury)* I'm curious. Just how did this disappearing diner trick start?

Mercury: It was an Illusion.

Mr. Pin: But how did it get started?

Mercury: *(Mercury twirls his long cape.)* I was sitting at the counter… *(harp music?)*

Mercury: *(Spreads out a deck of cards. A student is sitting next to him.)* Pick a card. *(Sally leaves a plate of cinnamon rolls next to the cards.)* I can make these cinnamon rolls disappear. *(He pulls out a scarf.)*

Acting friend: *(Taking a card)* Say, aren't you Mercury the Magician? *(The rolls disappear. Mercury could "find" them by one of the acting friends.)*

| Mercury | The same. And you are…? |
|---|---|
| Friend: | Lakesha. I know Maggie from school. I'm here with some acting students she knows. She told us a lot about the diner. We decided to see it for ourselves. |
| Mercury: | Do you know what's so great about this diner? |

Acting friend: The cinnamon rolls?

| Mercury: | Yes, of course those are very good. Seriously, Smiling Sally and Mr. Pin are what's best about this diner. They don't realize it though. |

Another friend: They should. The penguin detective is pretty famous. Maggie has told us about him. He has been her best friend for a long time.

| Mercury: | Pretty lucky to have a rockhopper penguin detective and Smiling Sally in your corner. |

Acting friend: They both help everyone. They never wait for a thanks. They just do another nice thing.

Another friend: *(whispering)* Shh… We don't want Sally and Mr. Pin to hear this. Maggie wants to show them both what they mean to her. She wants to have a play about Mr. Pin's cases and show what Aunt Sally does for people. Maggie asked us to help her with it and stage it right here in the diner.

Mercury: Good idea. Hmm. It's like a Wonderful Diner Life, or something like that.

Friend: Right. We could use your help. *(Then the friend whispers to Mercury.)*

Otis: I can offer elevator, pulley, and scaffolding expertise.

Mercury: Thank you, Otis. Most helpful. Yes, you have helped with some of my magic shows.

Maggie: We have to make sure that Sally and Mr. Pin don't get suspicious. Not easy in Mr. Pin's case.

Chorus: *(loud whisper)* He's on the case. *(harp music to transition)*

Sally: The diner just vanished.

Maggie:        I am so sorry about that. We had to get
               everyone out of the diner, so we could
               set it up for the surprise. We needed to
               make it disappear for just a little bit. A
               lot of people wanted to thank you and
               Mr. Pin for how you helped them. We
               thought a play would be the best way
               to show you.

O'Malley:      It was easy getting people to come.

Acting friend: And there were plenty of people who
               had stories to tell. The play just wrote
               itself, people remembering what Mr.
               Pin and Sally had done for them.

Maggie:        But I have to say, maybe I have the
               most to be thankful for. Mr. Pin, you
               and Sally helped me to be okay after
               my parents disappeared. Now I want
               to be a detective too.

Mr. Pin:       You are already a detective.

Acting friend: (to Maggie) Maggie the detective.
               Who is Brave.

Another friend: And strong.

| | |
|---|---|
| Luigi: | See what you've done for Maggie and all of us! Sally and Mr. Pin, you are clever and, above all, kind. It doesn't matter who you are or where you've been. Sally and Mr. Pin will help you. That's what you are all about. |
| Chorus: | Thank you! |
| Everyone: | You've been there for me, Aunt Sally, When I needed you, Aunt Sally, You took care of me, Since I was two. Without you, what would I do? You gave me gerbils, A CB radio, And you combed my curls. Made me cinnamon rolls, Oh, when I was all alone. You gave me a home, Aunt Sally. You've always been there, Aunt Sally. You took care of me, Aunt Sally, Since I was two. Without you, what would I do? |
| | Mr. Pin you've been our friend too, Always there when Chicago needs you. Without you, what would we do? |

Mercury: *(with a flourish of his cape)* And not all mysteries are crimes.

Mr. Pin: (Mr. Pin steps forward) Thank you all for coming. Drive safely. And remember, bad chocolate is always a crime.... Oh, and one more thing. I may be away for a little while. I have another very important mystery to solve. (Mr. Pin looks at Maggie.) Perhaps there is much more to the story about the disappearance of two dedicated scientists. Maggie's parents.

Chorus: Mr. Pin. Ra-da-da-da-da-da-da. He's on the case. Mr. Pin. Ra-da-da-da-da-da-da. He's on the case. Mr. Pin. Ra-da-da-da-da-da-da.

(whispered) He's on the case.

# Glossary

**armoire**    a tall cupboard or closet

**astounded**    amazed, shocked

**captivating**    holding interest

**catwalk**    a narrow walkway, usually used above a stage

**coincidence**    events happening by chance at the same time

**demolished**    torn down, destroyed

**diabolical**    bad, shocking

**distraction**    something that diverts attention

**glistened**    reflecting light, sparkling

**illumined**    lit up

**Murphy bed**    a bed that can be folded up into a wall closet

**permafrost**    arctic frozen soil

**salvaged**    saved property, furnishings

**scaffold**    structure used when building or repairing

**sconces**    wall light holder

**stout**    solid, hefty

**transformed**    changed

**Mr. Pin's** storied Chicago adventures began years ago when he literally hopped out of a bus and into Smiling Sally's Diner. He has been a detective ever since, more recently chasing a spy to South America. He has advanced degrees in criminal psychiatry and forensics from Lower Fahrenheit University. Current interests include climate change, fossils, magic, and chocolate. He continues to write his memoirs. This is the sixth book in that series.

**Maggie** continues her studies in Chicago. She attends a science school with a special interest in forensics. Maggie is thinking about being a detective one day. Mr. Pin says she is already a detective. She likes to read whenever she has a spare minute. When not away at school, she lives with her Aunt Sally above the diner on Monroe.

**Christina Cornier** began her art career at the age of three when she pulled her "Playschool" desk next to her father's and announced, "I am going to be an artist." Since then, her passion has grown and led to that childhood dream coming true. She received her BFA from the School of the Art Institute in Chicago and has exhibited her paintings internationally. Christina currently lives in Chicago, Illinois with her husband and an enigmatic cat. This is her second time illustrating a children's book.

**Mary Elise Monsell** authored many children's books, which were issued in several languages and reprints. Her Mr. Pin series, a bestseller in school book clubs and IRA/CBC Children's choice was developed into a musical in Chicago. Her UNDERWEAR book has become a classic. Mary has a bachelor's degree in journalism from Northwestern and a master's degree in teaching. She was a teacher in various settings for almost thirty years. She is thrilled to once again have talented artist Christina Cornier illustrate a new Mr. Pin.